Trans Dragon tattoo

Portraits of Trans Resilience

Eleanor Everly Rosewood

ISBN: 9798872737858

DEDICATION

To the resilient trans community,

This book is dedicated to each courageous soul navigating the intricate paths of self-discovery. "Trans Dragon Tattoo: Portraits of Trans Resilience" is a tribute to your strength, beauty, and unwavering spirit. In the dragon tattoos etched upon your skin, we find symbols of courage and resilience. May these pages stand as a mirror, reflecting your strength, and as a guiding light leading others toward understanding and acceptance. Your stories matter, your voices resonate, and your presence enriches the world.

With love and unwavering solidarity,

Eleanor Everly Rosewood

CONTENTS

TRANS TALES IN INK

"Trans Dragon Tattoo: Portraits of Trans Resilience" is a compelling coffee table book that showcases the striking beauty and individuality of trans individuals through the lens of their dragon tattoos. Each page is a visual celebration of identity and body art, bringing forth the unique stories and experiences of the featured individuals.

The book features a diverse collection of stunning portraits, each carefully crafted to emphasize the intricate details of the dragon tattoos that adorn the bodies of these resilient trans individuals. The dragon tattoos serve as powerful symbols, each telling a personal tale of strength, self-discovery, and the journey towards embracing their true identities.

Accompanying each portrait is a heartfelt poem that provides a glimpse into the individual's experiences and the significance of their dragon tattoo. These poems act as a poetic narrative, beautifully complementing the visual storytelling captured in the portraits. They delve into the intersection of identity and body art, offering readers an intimate understanding of the profound connection between the dragon tattoos and the trans sense of self.

"Trans Dragon Tattoo" goes beyond being a mere collection of portraits; it is a testament to the diverse and resilient experiences of the trans community. The dragon tattoos, showcased in all their glory, become visual representations of the strength and courage it takes to navigate the complexities of identity.

This coffee table book stands as a remarkable addition to the representation of diverse experiences, offering a space for trans individuals to see themselves reflected with pride and authenticity. "Trans Dragon Tattoo: Portraits of Trans Resilience" is an ode to self-expression, a celebration of identity, and a tribute to the beauty found in the intersection of body art and personal journeys.

CHAPTER 1

DRAGON STRENGTH AWAKENS

In ink and hues, Maya's tale unfurls,
Resilience, a symphony in the underworld.
Her canvas, a tapestry of courage spun,
A lotus whispers of battles won.
Within the dragon on her shoulder's crest,
Strength awakens, a silent protest.
Against the currents of societal streams,
Maya discovers the art of self-esteem.

In the calm of her gaze, serenity blooms,
A phoenix rises, dispelling inner gloom.
Stories written in lines and shade,
Maya's body, a testament to journeys made.
On her sleeve, a spectrum wide,
Pain and triumph interweave, side by side.
The hummingbird on her collarbone,
Dances in joy, a beauty all her own.

In the moonlit silence, our bodies intertwine,
A real desire, so beautifully designed.
Worshipping the trans body, a sacred art,
Every touch and caress, a masterpiece to impart.
Tasting the essence of love on our lips,
A real sensations, as desire equips.

Lustful whispers, desires set free,
In the sanctuary of love, just you and me.
Kissing with passion, a fiery embrace,
In the tender moments, love finds its place.

Making love like poetry, verses unfold,
A story of passion, beautifully told.
Reaching peaks of pleasure, ecstasy's peak,
Our bodies entangled, an intimate streak.

In the afterglow, a love so true,
An endless love making, just me and you.
In the stillness that follows, whispers remain,
Echoes of passion, a love that won't wane.

Sensual echoes of our intimate rhyme,
Entwined in the moment, transcending time.
The trans body, a shape of grace,
Each touch a testament, a tender embrace.

Kisses linger, a sweet aftertaste,
A love story written, no moment to waste.
Lustful gazes, a fiery connection,
A shared vulnerability, a profound reflection.
Bodies entangled, as love's tale unfolds,
In the silent language, our story holds.

Reveling in the aftermath, a tranquil glow,
Two souls connected, a fade and a flow.
In this dance of passion, a love pure and free,
Our journey continues, just you and me.

Maya's narrative, a tale profound,
Echoes of authenticity resound.
In the language of ink, a living art,
Each chapter etched on her brave heart.
Gaze into her eyes, and you'll find,
Maya's beauty, a melody, undefined.
A composition of courage, love, and grace,
In every stroke, a unique embrace.

In a quiet room, a haven of understanding,
Two souls converged, hearts gently landing.
A support group's embrace, a refuge so kind,
Where stories unfolded, the depths of the mind.
Amongst the circle, where acceptance blooms,
Two trans hearts found solace in shared rooms.
One bore a dragon, scales etched in ink,
A symbol of strength, in shadows it'd slink.

The other's dragon danced on skin so fair,
A silent companion, a guardian in air.
In this sacred space, their stories intertwined,
Of battles fought and the strength they'd find.
Eyes met across the room, a hesitant glance,
Two kindred spirits caught in fate's dance.
In the hush of confessions, they began to speak,
The dragon's silent language, strength unique.

"I carry a dragon," said one with a smile,
"A creature of fire, a symbol worthwhile.
It mirrors the flames that burned within,
A tale of rebirth, where life would begin."
The other nodded, a silent exchange,
Their dragon tattoos, a language so strange.
In the ink on their bodies, a shared history,
Of struggles and triumphs, a shared mystery.

Outside the group's walls, beneath the night sky,
Their connection deepened as stars drew them nigh.
A shared love for stargazing, a cosmic delight,
Brought them together in the soft moonlight.
They ventured to hills where darkness unveiled,
The canvas of the heavens, stars finely detailed.
Lying on blankets, side by side,
Their dragons on display, a source of pride.

As constellations whispered tales untold,
Two souls in awe, their hands tightly hold.
The dragon's fire mirrored in celestial hues,
The universe painting stories on their tattooed views.
In the quiet between spoken words,
A connection blossomed, like song from the birds.
The dragons on skin, a silent rapport,
Two trans hearts finding solace, wanting more.

Through the vastness of the cosmos, they roamed,
Exploring galaxies, hand in hand, they've flown.
The dragon's fire, a beacon in the night,
Guiding them through darkness, a shared light.
As dawn painted the sky with hues of gold,
They left the hillside, their story yet untold.

Two trans hearts, in each other they'd find,
Strength in their dragons, to the stars, they'd bind.
For in the quiet of the support group's room,
A connection sparked, transcending the gloom.
Two trans individuals, under stardust gleams,
Wove a tale of love with celestial themes.

Trans Dragon tattoo

In a quiet corner of a quaint bookstore's embrace,
Two souls converged, a meeting of time and space.
Two trans hearts, each carrying a dragon's might,
In the world of ink, their stories alight.

Shelves lined with tomes, wisdom untold,
Whispers of stories, secrets to behold.
One with a dragon, scales on their skin,
A tale of strength, where battles begin.

The other adorned with a dragon so grand,
A mythical guardian, a winged command.
In the quiet of pages, they found their retreat,
A sanctuary of words, where their stories would meet.

Amidst the paper-bound realms and leather-bound lore,
They shared their favorites, the tales they adore.
One spoke of dragons, of fire and flight,
The other of mysteries, hidden in the night.

In the poetry section, where verses cascaded,
They found a connection, their essence invaded.
Their dragons, silent witnesses to the literary dance,
In the world of books, a shared romance.
"I love the epics," said one with a grin,
"Of dragons and heroes, and battles to win.
Each page is a journey, a quest to be told,
In the inked realms, where dreams unfold."

The other nodded, a kindred spark,
In the world of books, where minds embark.
"I delve into mysteries, where shadows conspire,
In the dance of words, where truths transpire."
They roamed the aisles, side by side,
Lost in the tales, where worlds collide.
Their dragon tattoos, a silent decree,
In the pages of stories, their souls set free.

With each shared chapter, a connection was spun,
Two trans hearts, beneath the bookstore's sun.
In the fiction's embrace, their stories entwined,
In the realm of books, a friendship defined.
They lingered in history, and ventured through rhyme,
Shared laughter in romance, lost track of time.
Their dragons whispered in the quiet air,
A language of kinship, beyond compare.

Through fantasy landscapes and memoirs untold,
They traversed the bookstore, their haven of gold.
The dragons on skin, in the bookstore's embrace,
A silent dialogue, a poetic grace.
As the day waned, and the bookstore grew still,
They exchanged tales, the joy hard to distill.
Two trans hearts, bound by the written word,
In the quaint bookstore, their connection stirred.

Outside, the moon painted the sky with ink,
Two trans souls, in the bookstore's link.
Their dragon tattoos, symbols of might,
A shared love for books, an eternal light.
In the quiet of that quaint bookstore's nook,
Two trans individuals, their stories forsook.
For in the world of pages, they found a friend,
In the dance of dragons, their connection wouldn't end.

In the realm where dreams and reality intertwine,
Two trans friends embarked on an adventure divine.
A magical garden, a haven of enchantment,
Where flowers whispered secrets, a poetic enhancement.
Each friend adorned with a dragon's embrace,
In the language of ink, their stories would trace.
One dragon fierce, scales of vivid hue,
A symphony of colors, a breathtaking view.

Trans Dragon tattoo

The other's dragon, elegant and wise,
Wings stretched in wonder, under enchanted skies.
In the garden's embrace, their friendship grew,
A dance of dragons, a bond ever true.
Blossoms painted rainbows, a fragrant ballet,
As the two friends ventured, lost in the array.
Their dragon tattoos shimmered in the soft glow,
A silent conversation, a tale to bestow.

With every step, the magical garden unveiled,

A canvas of wonders, where dreams set sail.

The air, alive with whispers and laughter,

As the two friends wandered, their hearts growing fonder.

In the midst of wonders, a fountain did spring,

Its waters reflecting the joy they would bring.

Their dragon tattoos caught the shimmering light,

As they explored the garden, bathed in delight.

Butterflies danced in a kaleidoscope trance,
Around the two friends, a whimsical dance.
Their dragon tattoos stirred, alive with each flutter,
In the magical garden, their bond would utter.
As they strolled through meadows of luminescent blooms,
Their dragons conversed, dispelling all glooms.
Each flower they touched, a spell to unveil,
In the garden of magic, where stories set sail.

A rainbow bridge led to a tree of ancient lore,
Where the whispers of leaves held tales galore.
Their dragon tattoos glowed, a mystical sign,
In the heart of the garden, where fantasies entwine.
In the garden's heart, a labyrinth they'd find,
A maze of pathways, intricate and kind.
Their dragons led the way, with wisdom untold,
As they navigated the garden, bold and bold.

The sun dipped low, painting the sky in gold,
In the magical garden, their friendship would hold.
Underneath the moon, they sat by a fountain,
Their dragon tattoos shimmering, a radiant mountain.
The night sang lullabies, the stars overhead,
As the two friends rested, their worries shed.
In the magical garden, where dreams would align,
Their dragon tattoos glowed, a promise, a sign.

Through the twists and turns of the enchanted space,
Two trans friends explored, finding solace and grace.
Their dragons intertwined, tales forever spun,
In the magical garden, where the journey had begun.
As dawn kissed the petals, with hues so divine,
The friends left the garden, their souls in twine.
Their unique dragon tattoos, a mark of the quest,
In the book of their friendship, an eternal rest.

CHAPTER 2

THE DRAGON'S WHISPER

In the heart of the city's gentle hum,
Two trans souls sought refuge, their journey begun.
A rainy day, the world draped in gray,
They found solace in a cozy café.
The door chimed softly as they stepped inside,
Two figures seeking warmth, a haven to confide.
In the corner, where the rain's soft drumming met,
They found a table, a haven, a sanctuary set.

One with a dragon, scales of ancient lore,
Etched in ink, a guardian to adore.
The other's dragon danced with wings so wide,
A silent companion, a source of pride.
The aroma of coffee hung in the air,
As they settled into plush chairs with care.
The raindrops on the window, a dance so sweet,
As the two souls prepared for a chance to meet.

With every sip, the warmth unfurled,
A comforting melody in a coffee-filled world.
Their dragons on display, symbols so bold,
A silent language, a story to be told.
"I carry a dragon," said one with a smile,
"A creature fierce, a guardian, worthwhile.
In ink, the echoes of stories untold,
A tale of resilience, a narrative to hold."

The other nodded, a kindred exchange,
In the tattooed ink, a shared language.
"I too bear a dragon, in flight it gleams,
A symbol of strength, in the fabric of dreams."
As raindrops painted a soothing song,
The two trans hearts began to bond.
In the coffee shop's embrace, a camaraderie untold,
Their dragon tattoos spoke, in silence, so bold.

Outside, the world was veiled in mist,
But within the café, their connection persist.
Shared laughter and stories, a gentle rapport,
As they embraced the haven of the coffee shop's core.
The barista crafted lattes with care,
As the two friends exchanged stories to share.
Their dragons, silent witnesses to the scene,
In the cozy coffee shop, where moments convene.

Trans Dragon tattoo

The rain tapped softly on the windowpane,
As they shared dreams, transcending the mundane.
In the dance of conversations, in the coffee's heat,
Two trans souls found solace, their connection complete.
Through the window, the city's pulse they'd see,
Yet, within the café, it was just them, carefree.
Their dragon tattoos, reflections of strength,
A bond growing silently, in the coffee shop's length.

With every word, a new chapter unfurled,
In the cozy coffee shop, their friendship swirled.
The dragons on skin, stories intertwined,
A sanctuary found, in the warmth they'd find.
As the rain painted art on the glass,
They shared memories, a connection to amass.
The coffee shop's refuge, a refuge they'd keep,
Where two trans hearts found solace, in the rain's sweet sweep.

Trans Dragon tattoo

The hours passed like the slowest brew,
In the comforting haven where stories grew.
Their dragons, silent companions on this day,
In the cozy coffee shop, where friendship held sway.
The rain outside whispered tales of the past,
As the two friends in the café found peace at last.
Their dragon tattoos, in the soft café light,
A testament to the bond, so quiet, so bright.

And as the rain subsided, the city outside,
The two trans friends in the café did confide.
In the warmth of connection, a haven so sweet,
They left the cozy coffee shop, hearts replete.
The door chimed softly as they stepped into the mist,
Carrying the warmth of the café, where connections persist.
Their dragons whispered stories, in the city's ebb and flow,
Two trans hearts, finding solace, in the café's gentle glow.

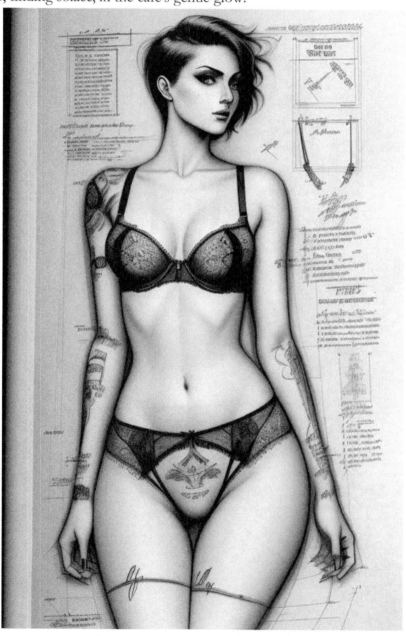

In a gallery aglow with vibrant hues,
Two trans souls met, a rendezvous.
A haven where art whispered tales untold,
Their stories woven in ink, a narrative to unfold.
One adorned with a dragon, scales so bold,
A canvas of strength, a story to be told.
The other's dragon soared on skin so fair,
Wings stretched in wonder, in the gallery's air.

Trans Dragon tattoo

Amidst the art, where colors would converse,
They found each other, a connection diverse.
Their dragons mirrored the strokes of the brush,
A silent dialogue, a shared artistic hush.
Paintings adorned the walls, a visual song,
A gallery of dreams where emotions throng.
In the dance of colors, their stories entwined,
Two trans hearts, a connection defined.

The first approached, with a smile so bright,
"Your dragon's tale, a captivating light.
In the inked strokes, a journey profound,
A silent narrative, in vibrant surround."
The second nodded, a kinship in art,
A shared appreciation from the soul's heart.
"Your dragon soars in colors so grand,
A visual symphony, across the skin's land."

They strolled through the gallery, brushstroke by brushstroke,
Admiring the art, where emotions awoke.
Their dragon tattoos, a testament to the art,
In the vibrant gallery, where connections start.
One pointed to a painting, colors ablaze,
"A masterpiece that reflects the sun's warm gaze.
My dragon, too, basks in this fiery light,
In the language of art, our stories unite."

The other smiled, tracing a dragon's flight,
On the canvas of skin, a visual delight.
"In this painting, I see a tale unfold,
A dragon's journey, in vibrant gold."
As they moved through the gallery's embrace,
They shared stories, their hearts set the pace.
Each painting a chapter, a tale to impart,
Their dragons echoed the strokes, a visual art.

In the impressionist realm, where colors blur,
They found a painting that made their hearts stir.
A dragon in soft strokes, a dreamlike sight,
In the gallery's silence, a shared delight.
In the surrealism corner, where reality bends,
A painting spoke of journeys with twists and bends.
Their dragons mirrored the surreal scene,
A connection formed, so vivid, so keen.

Trans Dragon tattoo

Through abstract canvases where chaos meets grace,
They explored the gallery, a wondrous space.
Their dragon tattoos, each stroke a decree,
In the language of art, their souls set free.
In the portrait section, eyes met eyes,
A connection formed, no need for disguise.
Their dragons whispered, a language so clear,
In the gallery's symphony, where emotions steer.

They lingered before a masterpiece, colors profound,
A dragon in harmony, a love newly found.
Their tattoos vibrated, a visual song,
In the gallery of art, where connections are strong.
As the gallery echoed with whispers untold,
They found a bench, a haven to hold.
Their dragons reflected in the gallery's light,
A silent conversation, a connection so bright.
In the quiet of the gallery's sanctuary,
Two trans souls found a bond visionary.

Their tattoos, inspired by the art they adore,
In the vibrant gallery, their connection did soar.
As they left the art-filled haven with grace,
They carried the gallery in each embrace.
Their dragons danced, a visual reverie,
Two trans hearts, connected in artistic decree.
In the world of ink and the canvas of skin,
Their story continued, a painting within.
A vibrant gallery, where connections take flight,
Two trans souls, in the tapestry of art and light.

Trans Dragon tattoo

Beneath the twilight's gentle embrace,
Two trans lovers found a tranquil space.
A lakeside haven, where ripples unfold,
Their hearts entwined, a story to be told.
One bore a dragon, scales in ink,
A symbol of strength, in shadows to sink.
The other adorned with a butterfly's grace,
Wings painted delicate, a dance in embrace.

In the soft glow of the moon's soft kiss,
They sought solace in a moment of bliss.
Their tattoos mirrored in the lake's reflection,
A silent ballet, a visual connection.
As the night unfolded its velvet wings,
They settled by the water, where the echo sings.
The dragon's fire, a quiet glow,
The butterfly's dance, a gentle flow.

Trans Dragon tattoo

The lake whispered tales of love untold,
As the two souls, in each other, strolled.
Their dragon and butterfly tattoos in play,
In the water's mirror, reflections at bay.
The dragon's scales shimmered, a moonlit sea,
A reflection of strength, of love so free.
The butterfly's wings, delicate and bright,
A reflection of freedom, taking flight.

Hand in hand, they sat by the lakeside,

A tender connection, love as their guide.

Their tattoos painted stories on the water's face,

In the stillness of the night, a tranquil embrace.

The dragon's gaze met the butterfly's flight,

In the quietude of the lake, under the moon's soft light.

Their love unfolded like petals unfurl,

A tale of connection, in a lakeside world.

They spoke not in words but in glances so deep,
As the lake held their secrets, the promises they'd keep.
The dragon and butterfly, reflections so clear,
In the water's embrace, a love sincere.
Whispers of the night echoed in the air,
As they shared stories, their hearts laid bare.
The dragon's fire and the butterfly's wing,
A symphony of love, as the night did sing.

Trans Dragon tattoo

The moon cast shadows, the water shimmered,
Their dragon and butterfly, their love undiminished.
A quiet moment, a lakeside ballet,
In the water's reflection, their love held sway.
As the night wore on and the stars convened,
The two lovers, beneath the moonlight gleaned,
Their tattoos danced in the water's reflection,
A love story etched, a heartfelt connection.

Trans Dragon tattoo

In the lakeside haven where silence spoke,
The dragon and butterfly, in love awoke.
A quiet moment, a timeless embrace,
Their souls entwined, in the lakeside grace.
As dawn painted the sky in hues of gold,
They left the lakeside, their story untold.
The dragon and butterfly, love's sweet tether,
In the tapestry of time, they'd dance forever.

CHAPTER 3

THE DRAGON'S FIRE

Through the emerald canopy, where sunlight weaves,
Two trans friends embarked on a journey, leaves beneath.
A challenging hike, trails winding and steep,
Their souls bound together, promises to keep.
One bore a dragon, scales fierce and grand,
In ink, tales of courage, etched on their skin, a brand.
The other's dragon danced with wings so wide,
A silent companion on this mountainous stride.

Trans Dragon tattoo

Underneath the azure sky, they began the ascent,
Two trans hearts, a journey both shared and meant.
The trail unfolded, a story underfoot,
Their dragon tattoos, symbols of the roots.
With each step, the mountain whispered tales,
The strength of their dragons, like steadfast sails.
The air grew thinner, the climb more steep,
But together they climbed, a promise to keep.

The dragon's scales glowed in the dappled light,
As the friends ascended, their spirits taking flight.
Wings spread wide, the other's dragon in tow,
A dance of strength, a mutual echo.
They navigated rocks, conquered the incline,
Their dragons mirrored in the mountain's design.
In the face of challenge, their spirits soared,
Two trans souls, in unity adored.

Trans Dragon tattoo

The wind whispered secrets, the trees bore witness,
As they climbed higher, their determination boundless.
Their dragon tattoos spoke a silent vow,
In the language of ink, a pact to avow.
As fatigue settled, and the trail grew steep,
They leaned on each other, promises to keep.
The dragon's fire, a beacon so bright,
Guiding them through the challenging height.

In the quiet pauses between breaths,
They found strength in the mountain's crests.
Their tattoos reflected in each other's gaze,
A testament to friendship that would amaze.
Through sweat and tears, laughter and strain,
They conquered the summit, the mountaintop gained.
Their dragons glowed, victorious and bold,
In the triumph of friendship, a tale to be told.
The view from the peak, breathtaking and vast,
Two trans hearts, a connection steadfast.
The dragon and dragonfly, symbols so profound,
In the vastness of nature, their friendship crowned.

As they descended, the trail winding down,
Their dragons echoed in the mountain's gown.
In the quiet descent, strength renewed,
Two trans friends, forever bonded, imbued.
At the base, as they stood side by side,
Their dragons reflected in the mountain's pride.
The challenging hike, a triumph complete,
In the language of tattoos, their friendship sweet.

Through the challenges faced on that mountainous trail,
Their friendship deepened, their spirits set sail.
The dragon's scales and the wings that soared,
In the tapestry of friendship, forever adored.
As they left the trail, the journey behind,
Their dragons whispered in the mountain wind.
Two trans souls, with strength anew,
A challenging hike, but their friendship true.

In the realm of melodies, where notes intertwine,
Two trans souls discovered a love divine.
A shared passion for music, a rhythm untold,
Their hearts beating in harmony, a story to unfold.
One bore a dragon, scales fierce and bright,
In ink, a visual symphony, a canvas of light.
The other's dragon danced with wings so wide,
A silent companion in the musical tide.

In the heart of a city's vibrant beat,
They met where melodies and echoes would meet.
A concert hall's embrace, a sanctuary of sound,
Their souls resonating, the connection profound.
The dragon's scales glimmered in the concert's glow,
As they embraced the music, a river to flow.
Wings stretched wide, the other's dragon in flight,
In the language of ink, a musical height.

Trans Dragon tattoo

Strings strummed and drums reverberated,
Their dragons stirred, the notes coordinated.
A shared passion, a love for the song,
In the symphony of life, where they belonged.
They spoke not in words but in musical notes,
The language of their hearts, in rhythm it floats.
Their dragons echoed the melodies they heard,
In the language of ink, a shared concord.

In the quiet interludes between the beats,
They shared stories, their hearts on repeat.
The dragon's fire and the wings' gentle sway,
In the language of tattoos, their connection at play.
As the music flowed, emotions cascading,
They found solace in the notes parading.
Their dragons mirrored the tunes so sweet,
In the concert hall's warmth, where melodies meet.

In the encore's echo, they ventured outside,
Their dragons alive in the city's night.
In the glow of streetlights and neon signs,
Two trans hearts danced, their spirits entwined.
In a quiet café, where the night met dawn,
They sat, their love for music lingering on.
Their dragon tattoos, symbols so grand,
In the language of ink, a musical strand.

With each shared song, a connection grew,
Their dragons whispered, the notes they knew.
A musical bond, a friendship so rare,
In the city's heartbeat, a symphony to share.
As the sun painted the sky in hues of gold,
They left the café, their story to be told.
Their dragon tattoos, in the dawn's soft glow,
A testament to the musical love they'd stow.
Through the city's streets, they walked hand in hand,
Their dragons reflected in the morning's brand.
A shared passion for music, a journey anew,
Two trans souls, in a melody true.

Trans Dragon tattoo

As the world awakened to a brand-new day,
Their music-infused connection held sway.
The dragon's fire and the wings' gentle flight,
In the language of tattoos, a bond taking flight.
In the symphony of life, where notes entwine,
Two trans hearts found a melody divine.
A shared passion for music, a love so grand,
Expressed through dragon tattoos, forever to stand.

CHAPTER 4

TRANS CONNECTION GROWING

In a kitchen aglow with warmth and light,
Two trans souls converged, their spirits taking flight.
A shared love for cooking, a culinary embrace,
Their hearts in rhythm, a dance to trace.
One bore a dragon, scales fierce and bold,
In ink, a symbol of strength, a story to be told.
The other's dragon danced with wings so wide,
A silent companion in the kitchen's tide.

Trans Dragon tattoo

In the realm of flavors, where ingredients play,
They discovered their shared passion one fateful day.
Their dragon tattoos, a culinary decree,
In the language of ink, a shared jubilee.
With aprons adorned, they stood side by side,
A kitchen tableau, where dreams would abide.
Their dragons whispered in the simmering air,
As they embarked on a culinary affair.

The chopping board echoed with rhythmic beats,
As they prepared ingredients, their hearts in feats.
The dragon's scales shimmered in the kitchen's glow,
A visual feast, the ink's vibrant show.
Together they diced, and together they laughed,
Their dragons in harmony, a culinary craft.
The dance of spices, a symphony of smells,
In the kitchen's haven, where friendship swells.

Trans Dragon tattoo

One stirred the pot, while the other would taste,
A fusion of flavors, no element to waste.
Their dragons surveyed, guardians so grand,
In the culinary journey, where they'd stand.
Aromas of herbs and spices took flight,
As they conjured a feast, a culinary delight.
Their dragon tattoos, reflections in the pan,
A tale in each dish, a part of their plan.

Trans Dragon tattoo

In the sizzle of pans and the simmering stew,
They exchanged stories, their connection grew.
The dragon's fire and the wings' gentle sweep,
In the kitchen's alchemy, a friendship to keep.
They rolled out dough with laughter and grace,
Creating memories in that culinary space.
Their dragon tattoos, a testament to the day,
In the art of cooking, where passions lay.

As the oven hummed and the flavors melded,
They plated their creation, the masterpiece unveiled.
Their dragons glistened, a culinary twine,
In the tapestry of taste, where moments entwine.
With candles aglow and the table adorned,
They sat down together, a friendship adorned.
The feast before them, a triumph of connection,
Their dragon tattoos, a visual confection.
In the shared joy of each flavorful bite,
They celebrated the culinary night.
Their dragons whispered in the afterglow,
A bond forged in the kitchen's flow.

Trans Dragon tattoo

As the evening waned and stars did gleam,
They left the kitchen, a culinary dream.
Their dragon tattoos, in the moon's soft light,
A testament to the feast, to the shared delight.
Through the tapestry of friendship and flavors so grand,
Two trans souls found connection, a culinary strand.
In the kitchen's embrace, where stories unfold,
Their dragon tattoos, in the culinary journey, forever told.

Trans Dragon tattoo

In the middle of the city's heartbeat, where dreams unfold,
Two trans souls navigated the streets of gold.
In the hustle and bustle, where life would surge,
They found courage and love, a passionate verge.
One bore a dragon, scales fierce and bright,
In ink, a symbol of sensuality, a story to ignite.
The other's dragon danced with wings so wide,
A silent companion in the city's stride.

Through neon-lit streets and avenues alive,
They explored the city, where passions would thrive.
Their dragon tattoos, a narrative untold,
In the language of ink, a sensuous mold.
In the city's rhythm, where desires entwine,
They discovered a courage, a love so divine.
Their dragons whispered tales of vulnerability,
In the dance of shadows, a shared sensuality.

Trans Dragon tattoo

As they strolled through the city's vibrant nights,
Their dragons shimmered in the neon lights.
Wings stretched wide, scales aglow,
In the language of tattoos, a passion to show.
In a jazz-filled bar, where saxophones wailed,
They found a haven where love set sail.
Their dragon tattoos, reflections in the dim,
In the city's embrace, a sensuous hymn.

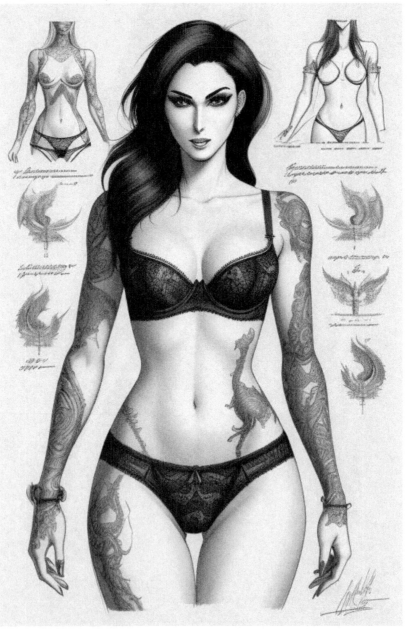

The night unfolded in a sultry trance,
As they danced together, a serendipitous chance.
Their dragons entwined, a visual duet,
In the city's heartbeat, where passions met.
Through the whispers of the city's nocturnal air,
They shared stories, vulnerabilities laid bare.
Their dragon tattoos, a symbol of might,
In the language of ink, a shared delight.

Trans Dragon tattoo

As dawn painted the city in hues so bold,
They wandered through streets of stories untold.
Their dragons whispered in the morning light,
A connection forged in the city's bright.
In the quietude of a coffee shop's charm,
They sat, hearts open, safe from harm.
Their dragon tattoos, a display so bold,
In the city's warmth, a love story to be told.

Through the tapestry of city lights and lore,
They found courage, love, and so much more.
Their dragons on skin, a testament to the night,
In the city's heartbeat, where love took flight.
In the intimacy of their shared vulnerability,
They embraced the city's sensual sensibility.
Their dragon tattoos, symbols of passion and grace,
In the city's embrace, a love to chase.

As they left the city's embrace, hand in hand,
Their dragons spoke of a love so grand.
Through the urban tapestry, a tale unfurls,
Two trans hearts, in the city, found pearls.
In the rhythm of the city, where desires ignite,
They discovered courage and love in the night.
Their dragon tattoos, in the morning's glow,
A testament to sensuality, in the city's ebb and flow.

CHAPTER 5

TRANSCENDENT DRAGONS

In a room bathed in the soft glow of creativity's light,
Two trans souls converged, where poetry took flight.
A poetry workshop, a haven for words to be spun,
Their hearts beating in rhythm, a duet begun.
One bore a dragon, scales fierce and grand,
In ink, a symbol of strength, a tale to withstand.
The other's skin adorned with verses so fine,
A dance of words, where emotions entwine.

As they sat amidst pages and ink-stained delight,
Their dragon tattoos reflected the workshop's light.
Wings stretched wide, scales aglow,
In the language of ink, a poetic show.
In the realm of stanzas, where metaphors play,
They found connection, words weaving a way.
Their dragon tattoos, a silent rapport,
In the world of poetry, a connection to explore.

"I carry a dragon," said one with a grin,
"In the verses I write, its tales begin.
A creature of fire, strength so vast,
In the world of words, where emotions contrast."
The other nodded, a kindred exchange,
Their poetry echoed, a shared range.
"I ink verses on my skin," the response sincere,
"In the dance of words, where dreams appear."

As the workshop unfolded, the verses took shape,
Each line a brushstroke, emotions to drape.
Their dragon tattoos, symbols so bold,
In the poetry workshop, where stories are told.
They penned verses that spoke of strength,
Of dragons in flight, covering length.
Their tattoos mirrored the verses they'd write,
A poetic dialogue, in the workshop's light.

Through sonnets and ballads, emotions explored,
They discovered connections, stories adored.
The dragon's fire and the verses' sway,
In the poetry workshop, a bond held sway.
In the quiet interludes, between written lines,
They shared stories, where the heart refines.
Their dragon tattoos, reflections in the ink,
In the world of poetry, a connection to link.

Through the rhythm of verses and the workshop's beat,
They found solace, their stories complete.
The dragon's gaze and the verses' might,
In the language of poetry, a connection so bright.
As the workshop concluded, in the fading light,
They left with verses, a bond taking flight.
Their dragon tattoos, a visual accord,
In the world of poetry, where connections are stored.

Through the tapestry of words and ink,
Two trans hearts found a connection to link.
Their dragon tattoos, a silent embrace,
In the poetry workshop, a friendship to trace.
As they ventured beyond the workshop's door,
Their verses echoed, a connection to explore.
The dragon's fire and the words' embrace,
In the world of poetry, where connections find grace.

Trans Dragon tattoo

In a studio of mirrors, where the dance began,
Two trans souls converged, their journey to span.
A dance class, a realm of movement and grace,
Their hearts entwined, in the studio's embrace.
One bore a dragon, scales fierce and bright,
In ink, a symbol of movement, a story in flight.
The other's dragon danced with wings so wide,
A silent partner, in the dance class's tide.

As they stepped onto the floor, a rhythmic start,
Their dragon tattoos, a dance of the heart.
Wings stretched wide, scales aglow,
In the language of ink, a ballet to show.
The instructor guided, as music took hold,
Two trans hearts, in a dance story to unfold.
Their dragon tattoos, reflections in the mirror,
In the dance of movement, a connection to revere.

In the waltz of motion, where challenges arose,
They found courage, where confidence grows.
The dragon's gaze and the dance's swirl,
In the dance class's rhythm, a shared twirl.
Through pirouettes and leaps, they navigated,
Their dragon tattoos, in the studio's symphony created.
In the language of movement, a ballet so bright,
In the dance class's challenge, their connection took flight.

"I carry a dragon," said one with a grin,
"In every step, its tales begin.
A creature of grace, in the dance so divine,
In the world of movement, where stories entwine."
The other nodded, a kindred exchange,
Their dragon tattoos, in the studio's range.
"I too bear a dragon, in flight it gleams,
A symbol of movement, in the dance of dreams."

As the class progressed, their movements refined,
Their dragons whispered, in the studio's mind.
Wings stretched wide, scales glistening,
In the language of movement, a connection listening.
In the quiet pauses between dance and reprieve,
They shared stories, their hearts did weave.
The dragon's fire and the dance's grace,
In the dance class's haven, a connection to embrace.

Through the waltz of challenges and the ballet's trance,
They found solace in each other's dance.
Their dragon tattoos, a testament so bold,
In the language of movement, a story to be told.
In the studio's rhythm, where dreams take hold,
They discovered a bond, a connection so bold.
The dragon's wings and the dance's art,
In the dance class's sanctuary, a connection to chart.
As the music softened and the class drew near an end,
They left the studio, a newfound friend.

Trans Dragon tattoo

Their dragon tattoos, in the dance's glow,
A testament to movement, in the stories they'd show.
Through the challenges faced on the studio's floor,
Their friendship deepened, their spirits soared.
The dragon's fire and the dance's embrace,
In the tapestry of movement, a connection to trace.
As they ventured beyond the dance class's door,
Their movements echoed, a connection to explore.
The dragon's gaze and the dance's embrace,
In the world of movement, where connections find grace.

CHAPTER 6

THE SYMBOL OF STRENGTH

Beneath the canvas of a star-strewn night,
Two trans lovers sought a tranquil sight.
A hammock swaying in a gentle breeze,
Their haven of comfort, where hearts found ease.
One bore a dragon, scales vivid and grand,
In ink, a symbol of strength, a story to withstand.
The other's dragon danced with wings so wide,
A silent companion in the celestial tide.

Trans Dragon tattoo

As they nestled in the hammock's gentle swing,
Their dragon tattoos, in the moonlight would sing.
Wings stretched wide, scales aglow,
In the language of ink, a celestial show.
The hammock cradled them, a cocoon of grace,
As stars above painted the night's embrace.
Their dragons shimmered in the soft night air,
A visual symphony, a love affair.

The night unfolded with stories untold,
In the hammock's sway, love would unfold.
Their dragon tattoos whispered in the breeze,
In the quiet of the night, where dreams find ease.
As they gazed at the stars, their fingers entwined,
Their dragon tattoos, a love note designed.
Wings stretched wide, scales so bright,
In the hammock's cocoon, a celestial light.

"I carry a dragon," said one with a smile,
"In the ink, its tales stretch a mile.
A creature of fire, in the night it gleams,
A guardian of dreams, in celestial dreams."
The other nodded, a kindred exchange,
Their dragon tattoos, a love language so strange.
"I too bear a dragon, in flight it gleams,
A symbol of love, in the realm of dreams."

In the quiet of the hammock's gentle swing,
They shared stories, a love offering.
The dragon's fire and the wings' gentle sweep,
In the celestial hammock, their connection deep.
Through the whispers of the night, a serenade,
They found comfort in the hammock's shade.
Their dragon tattoos, in the moonlight's glow,
A testament to love, in the celestial show.

Trans Dragon tattoo

As the night wore on, the hammock held fast,
Their love growing, a bond unsurpassed.
The dragon's gaze and the stars' bright gleam,
In the hammock's cradle, a celestial dream.
Under the vast tapestry of the cosmic sea,
They whispered love, wild and free.
Their dragon tattoos, in the night's soft sway,
A visual poem, a love display.
In the hammock's gentle swing, they lay,
Under the stars, where dreams hold sway.

The dragon's fire and the wings' caress,
In the hammock's haven, a love fortress.
As dawn painted the sky in hues so divine,
They left the hammock, their love enshrined.
Their dragon tattoos, in the morning light,
A symbol of love, under the stars so bright.
Through the tapestry of time, their love would soar,
In the hammock's embrace, forevermore.
The dragon's gaze and the stars' soft hum,
In the celestial love story, where two hearts become one.

In the heart of a vibrant community's cheer,
Two trans souls joined a project dear.
A party in motion, a celebration so grand,
Their journey entwined, in the community's land.
One bore a dragon, scales fierce and bright,
In ink, a symbol of growth, a story taking flight.
The other's dragon danced with wings so wide,
A silent companion in the community's stride.

As they embraced the festivities, joy abound,
Their dragon tattoos, symbols profound.
Wings stretched wide, scales aglow,
In the language of ink, a community's show.
The party project blossomed with each passing day,
Their dragons mirrored the growth, in a visual display.
In the dance of colors, where dreams unfurl,
Two trans hearts, in the community swirl.

The dragon's scales shimmered in the festive light,
As they contributed to the project, hearts alight.
Wings stretched wide, the other's dragon in tow,
A dance of creation, in the community's flow.
"I carry a dragon," said one with a grin,
"In the ink, its tales of growth begin.
A creature of strength, in the community's embrace,
A guardian of dreams, in this vibrant space."

The other nodded, a kindred exchange,
Their dragon tattoos, in the community's range.
"I too bear a dragon, in flight it gleams,
A symbol of growth, in the realm of dreams."
As the project unfolded, their contributions grew,
Their dragons whispered, in the community's view.
Wings stretched wide, scales so bright,
In the language of ink, a communal light.

Through laughter and stories, their connections deepened,
Their dragon tattoos, in the community's keeping.
In the dance of collaboration, where dreams intertwine,
Two trans souls found a community so fine.
In the quiet moments, between the cheers,
They shared stories, where growth appears.
The dragon's fire and the wings' gentle sweep,
In the community's project, their connection deep.

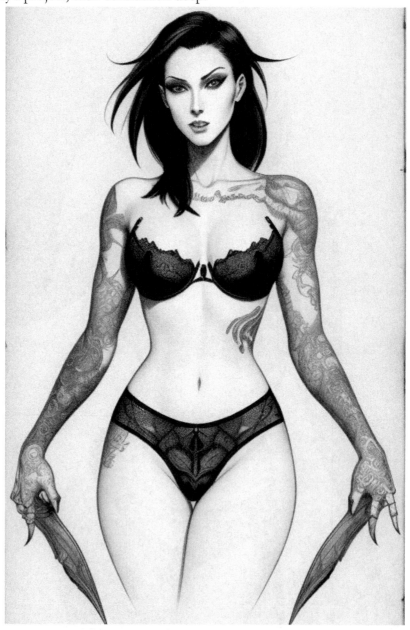

Through the tapestry of colors and artistic delight,
They witnessed the growth, a shared insight.
Their dragon tattoos, reflections of the day,
In the community's celebration, where dreams held sway.
As the project neared its festive end,
They looked at their dragons, a message to send.
Wings stretched wide, scales so bright,
In the language of ink, a community's light.

Trans Dragon tattoo

Through the tapestry of growth and connections so true,
Two trans hearts found a community to imbue.
The dragon's gaze and the project's bloom,
In the celebration, where dreams find room.
As they left the community's festive cheer,
Their dragons echoed, a message clear.
In the dance of colors and growth so grand,
Two trans souls, forever part of the community's land.

Upon the shores of memories, where waves embrace,
Two trans souls met, reuniting in a timeless space.
Years had passed, like the tides' ebb and flow,
Their hearts entwined, where the sea breezes blow.
One bore a dragon, scales vivid and bright,
In ink, a symbol of time, a story taking flight.
The other's dragon danced with wings so wide,
A silent companion in the reunion's tide.

As they stood on the beach, where the sands recall,
Their dragon tattoos reflected the waves, standing tall.
Wings stretched wide, scales aglow,
In the language of ink, a reunion to show.
The ocean echoed tales of journeys untold,
As they embraced, a connection to unfold.
Their dragons whispered in the salty air,
A visual symphony, a reunion so rare.

Trans Dragon tattoo

"I carry a dragon," said one with a smile,
"In the ink, its tales stretch a mile.
A creature of time, in the waves it gleams,
A guardian of memories, in the sea of dreams."
The other nodded, a kindred exchange,
Their dragon tattoos, a reunion's range.
"I too bear a dragon, in flight it gleams,
A symbol of time, in the realm of dreams."

Trans Dragon tattoo

As they walked along the shoreline, memories in tow,
Their dragons mirrored the waves' rhythmic flow.
Wings stretched wide, scales so bright,
In the language of ink, a reunion's light.
Through the whispers of the ocean breeze,
They shared stories, where the heart agrees.
The dragon's fire and the wings' gentle sweep,
In the reunion's moment, memories deep.

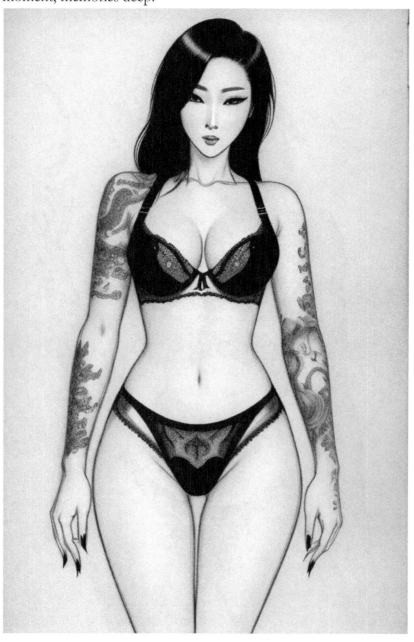

Through the tapestry of time, where moments replay,
They discovered connection, as waves decay.
Their dragon tattoos, reflections in the sand,
A testament to the reunion, where dreams expand.
As the sun dipped low and painted the sky,
They sat on the beach, where seagulls fly.
Their dragons glistening, a visual rhyme,
In the reunion's embrace, transcending time.

Trans Dragon tattoo

In the quiet of the evening, as stars did gleam,
They spoke of the years, the journey, the dream.
The dragon's gaze and the waves' soft hum,
In the reunion's silence, where two hearts become one.
Through the sands of time, where footprints fade,
They left the beach, memories laid.
Their dragon tattoos, in the moon's soft glow,
A reunion's testament, a love to bestow.
Through the tapestry of reunion, where memories find grace,
Two trans souls walked, embraced.
The dragon's wings and the waves' soft chime,
In the reunion's echo, transcending time.

CHAPTER 7

THRONE OF TRANS RESILIENCE

In the realm of threads from eras bygone,
Two trans friends embarked on a fashion dawn.
Vintage treasures and garments with tales,
Their hearts entwined, where the past unveils.
One bore a dragon, scales vivid and bright,
In ink, a symbol of style, a story to ignite.
The other's dragon danced with wings so wide,
A silent companion in the vintage tide.

As they scoured thrift stores, a treasure trove,
Their dragon tattoos added flair, a visual stove.
Wings stretched wide, scales aglow,
In the language of ink, a vintage show.
The fabrics whispered tales of days of old,
As they explored the racks, their stories unfold.
Their dragons shimmered, a visual feast,
In the vintage haven, where styles increased.

"I carry a dragon," said one with a grin,
"In the ink, its tales of style begin.
A creature of flair, in the fabric it gleams,
A guardian of vintage dreams."
The other nodded, a kindred exchange,
Their dragon tattoos, in the vintage range.
"I too bear a dragon, in flight it gleams,
A symbol of style, in the realm of dreams."
As they tried on dresses with frills so grand,
Their dragons reflected in the mirrors' stand.

Wings stretched wide, scales so bright,
In the language of ink, a vintage delight.
Through the tapestry of styles, where decades blend,
They found solace in fashion, a friendship to mend.
The dragon's gaze and the fabrics' embrace,
In the vintage world, their connection took place.
In the quiet corners of the vintage store,
They shared stories, where styles adore.
The dragon's fire and the fabrics' sway,
In the vintage symphony, a friendship to convey.

Through the echoes of fashion's timeless tune,
They danced through decades under the vintage moon.
Their dragon tattoos, in the changing room's glow,
A testament to style, where stories bestow.
As they left the store, bags in hand,
Their vintage treasures, a friendship to withstand.
Wings stretched wide, scales so bright,
In the language of ink, a vintage night.

Trans Dragon tattoo

Through the streets where fashion meets time,
They showcased their finds, a fashion mime.
Their dragon tattoos, in the sunlight's gleam,
A symbol of vintage style, a friendship's dream.
In the cafes where jazz tunes played,
They sipped coffee, vintage dreams conveyed.
The dragon's gaze and the styles' gentle sway,
In the vintage rhythm, their friendship held sway.

Through the tapestry of styles and eras so grand,
Two trans souls found connection in fashion's hand.
The dragon's wings and the fabrics' might,
In the vintage love story, where friendship takes flight.
As the sun set on the vintage day,
They walked through the streets, where memories lay.
Their dragon tattoos, in the evening light,
A vintage connection, transcending time.

In a hall where echoes of silence prevailed,
Two trans souls, their stories untold, unveiled.
A public speaking event, a challenge embraced,
Their hearts in tandem, courage interlaced.
One bore a dragon, scales vivid and bright,
In ink, a symbol of courage, a story taking flight.
The other's dragon danced with wings so wide,
A silent companion in the public-speaking tide.

As they stood before the audience's gaze,
Their dragon tattoos, a testament ablaze.
Wings stretched wide, scales aglow,
In the language of ink, a courage to show.
The stage, a daunting landscape, vast and grand,
Yet side by side, they took a stand.
Their dragons whispered in the hushed air,
A visual symphony, a courage to declare.

"I carry a dragon," said one with a grin,
"In the ink, its tales of courage begin.
A creature of strength, in the stories it gleams,
A guardian of resilience, in the realm of dreams."
The other nodded, a kindred exchange,
Their dragon tattoos, in the courage range.
"I too bear a dragon, in flight it gleams,
A symbol of bravery, in the realm of dreams."

As they spoke, their voices strong and clear,
Their dragons mirrored, a courage sincere.
Wings stretched wide, scales so bright,
In the language of ink, a courage's light.
Through the tapestry of words, where fears dissolve,
They found strength in each other's resolve.
The dragon's gaze and the words' gentle sway,
In the public-speaking realm, courage held sway.

Trans Dragon tattoo

In the quiet pauses between spoken lines,
They shared stories, where courage intertwines.
The dragon's fire and the words' embrace,
In the public-speaking space, a connection to trace.
Through the audience's gaze, where judgments loom,
They found solace in each other's room.
Their dragon tattoos, reflections in the applause,
A testament to courage, in the audience's cause.

As the event concluded, applause cascading,
They left the stage, their courage not fading.
Wings stretched wide, scales so bright,
In the language of ink, a courage-filled night.
Through the streets where city lights gleamed,
They walked, their courage forever deemed.
Their dragon tattoos, in the moon's soft glow,
A symbol of bravery, in the courage they'd show.

Trans Dragon tattoo

Through the tapestry of courage and spoken words,
Two trans souls found strength in each other's chords.
The dragon's wings and the words' gentle might,
In the courage-filled journey, where friendship takes flight.
As they ventured beyond the spotlight's embrace,
Their courage echoed in the city's space.
The dragon's gaze and the words' soft hum,
In the realm of courage, where two hearts become one.

Beneath the veil of the twilight sky,
Two trans lovers beneath the lanterns lie.
A festival aglow with lanterns so bright,
Their hearts entwined, like stars in the night.
One bore a dragon, scales vivid and grand,
In ink, a symbol of love, a story to withstand.
The other's dragon danced with wings so wide,
A silent companion in the lantern-lit tide.

As they strolled through the festival's embrace,
Their dragon tattoos, like lanterns, found grace.
Wings stretched wide, scales aglow,
In the language of ink, a love to show.
The lanterns above painted the night,
A canvas of colors, a festival's light.
Their dragons shimmered, a visual delight,
In the lantern-lit haven, where love takes flight.

The festival whispered tales of dreams,
As they wandered, hand in hand, it seems.
Their dragons echoed, a love so rare,
In the lantern-lit magic, a connection to share.
"I carry a dragon," said one with a smile,
"In the ink, its tales of love stretch a mile.
A creature of passion, in the lanterns it gleams,
A guardian of dreams, in the realm of dreams."

The other nodded, a kindred exchange,
Their dragon tattoos, in the lantern range.
"I too bear a dragon, in flight it gleams,
A symbol of love, in the realm of dreams."
As they strolled amidst lanterns that sway,
Their dragons mirrored the festival's display.
Wings stretched wide, scales so bright,
In the language of ink, a love's soft light.

Through the tapestry of lantern-lit trails,
They found solace in love's sweet tales.
The dragon's gaze and the lanterns' soft glow,
In the festival's warmth, a love to show.
In the quiet moments, between lanterns' gleam,
They shared stories, where love's dreams teem.
The dragon's fire and the lanterns' sway,
In the lantern-lit realm, their love held sway.

Through the sea of lanterns, a river so grand,
They danced and laughed, hand in hand.
Their dragon tattoos, reflections in the night,
A testament to love, in the lanterns' light.
As the festival waned, and stars took flight,
They left, hearts aglow, a love so bright.
Wings stretched wide, scales so bright,
In the language of ink, a lantern-lit night.

Through the streets where lanterns still gleamed,
They walked, their love forever esteemed.
Their dragon tattoos, in the moon's soft glow,
A symbol of love, in the lantern-lit show.
Through the tapestry of love, where lanterns align,
Two trans hearts found a connection divine.
The dragon's wings and the lanterns' soft hum,
In the lantern-lit festival, where love becomes one.

CHAPTER 8

TRANS SOARING: WHERE DREAMS TAKE FLIGHT

Beneath the velvet canvas of the midnight sky,
Two trans friends beneath the cosmos lie.
A telescope poised, stars like diamonds above,
Their hearts entwined, in a celestial love.
One bore a dragon, scales vivid and grand,
In ink, a symbol of dreams, a story to withstand.
The other's dragon danced with wings so wide,
A silent companion in the stargazing tide.

As they set up the telescope, a cosmic dance,
Their dragon tattoos, like constellations, enhance.
Wings stretched wide, scales aglow,
In the language of ink, a celestial show.
The telescope whispered tales of distant spheres,
As they explored the galaxies, eyes brimming with tears.
Their dragons shimmered, a visual delight,
In the stargazing haven, where dreams take flight.

"I carry a dragon," said one with a grin,
"In the ink, its tales of the cosmos begin.
A creature of wonder, in the stars it gleams,
A guardian of dreams, in the realm of dreams."
The other nodded, a kindred exchange,
Their dragon tattoos, in the stargazing range.
"I too bear a dragon, in flight it gleams,
A symbol of dreams, in the realm of dreams."

As they peered through the telescope's lens,
Their dragons reflected the cosmic trends.
Wings stretched wide, scales so bright,
In the language of ink, a celestial light.
Through the tapestry of stars, where stories unfold,
They found solace in the mysteries untold.
The dragon's gaze and the galaxies' soft glow,
In the stargazing haven, a connection to sow.

In the quiet moments between each constellation,
They shared stories, a celestial conversation.
The dragon's fire and the stars' gentle sway,
In the stargazing sanctuary, their connection lay.
Through the sea of stars, a cosmic sea so grand,
They delved into the wonders, hand in hand.
Their dragon tattoos, reflections in the night,
A testament to the cosmos, in the stargazing light.
As the night wore on, and meteors streaked,
They left the telescope, their spirits peaked.

Wings stretched wide, scales so bright,
In the language of ink, a celestial night.
Through the fields where moonlight gleamed,
They walked, their dreams forever esteemed.
Their dragon tattoos, in the moon's soft glow,
A symbol of wonder, in the stargazing show.
Through the tapestry of dreams, where galaxies align,
Two trans hearts found a celestial sign.
The dragon's wings and the stars' soft hum,
In the stargazing journey, where friendship becomes one.

Trans Dragon tattoo

In a space adorned with blank walls, a canvas vast,
Two trans souls stood, identity unsurpassed.
A mural awaiting, a masterpiece to create,
Their hearts entwined, in the artistry of fate.
One bore a dragon, scales vivid and grand,
In ink, a symbol of identity, a story to withstand.
The other's dragon danced with wings so wide,
A silent companion in the mural tide.

As they dipped their brushes in colors so bright,
Their dragon tattoos mirrored the creative light.
Wings stretched wide, scales aglow,
In the language of ink, a mural to show.
The canvas whispered tales of expression so bold,
As they painted, identities to unfold.
Their dragons shimmered, a visual delight,
In the mural's embrace, where colors ignite.

"I carry a dragon," said one with a grin,
"In the ink, its tales of identity begin.
A creature of courage, in the colors it gleams,
A guardian of self, in the realm of dreams."
The other nodded, a kindred exchange,
Their dragon tattoos, in the mural range.
"I too bear a dragon, in flight it gleams,
A symbol of self, in the realm of dreams."

As they blended hues in a collaborative dance,
Their dragons reflected the mural's expanse.
Wings stretched wide, scales so bright,
In the language of ink, a mural's light.
Through the tapestry of colors, where stories blend,
They found solace in the art, a connection to send.
The dragon's gaze and the mural's gentle sway,
In the creative sanctuary, their identities lay.

In the quiet moments between strokes of art,
They shared stories, where identities impart.
The dragon's fire and the mural's gentle grace,
In the collaborative canvas, a connection to trace.
Through the strokes and splatters of colors so grand,
They painted a mural, hand in hand.
Their dragon tattoos, reflections in the paint,
A testament to identity, where stories acquaint.

As the mural neared completion, a visual delight,
They stepped back, identities in the mural's light.
Wings stretched wide, scales so bright,
In the language of ink, a mural's night.
Through the space where artistry gleamed,
They walked, their identities forever esteemed.
Their dragon tattoos, in the mural's soft glow,
A symbol of self, in the artistic flow.
Through the tapestry of identities, where colors align,
Two trans souls found a connection divine.
The dragon's wings and the mural's soft hum,
In the collaborative masterpiece, where identity becomes one.

CHAPTER 9

TRANSCENDENT WILDERNESS: NAVIGATING THE TIDE

Beneath the canopy of a forest so vast,
Two trans souls sought refuge, a camping repast.
Nature's embrace, a sanctuary so grand,
Their hearts entwined, in the wild they'd stand.
One bore a dragon, scales vivid and bright,
In ink, a symbol of strength, a story to ignite.
The other's dragon danced with wings so wide,
A silent companion in the wilderness tide.

As they set up camp, amidst trees so tall,
Their dragon tattoos, symbols of the wilderness call.
Wings stretched wide, scales aglow,
In the language of ink, a forest tableau.
The wilderness whispered tales of ancient lore,
As they ventured deeper, their spirits soared.
Their dragons shimmered, a visual delight,
In the camping haven, where stars ignite.

"I carry a dragon," said one with a grin,
"In the ink, its tales of strength begin.
A creature of the wild, in the forest it gleams,
A guardian of courage, in the realm of dreams."
The other nodded, a kindred exchange,
Their dragon tattoos, in the wilderness range.
"I too bear a dragon, in flight it gleams,
A symbol of resilience, in the realm of dreams."
As they hiked through trails, where shadows play,
Their dragons mirrored the forest's display.
Wings stretched wide, scales so bright,
In the language of ink, a wilderness light.

Through the tapestry of trees, where secrets unfold,
They found solace in nature, a story to be told.
The dragon's gaze and the forest's gentle sway,
In the wilderness sanctuary, their connection lay.
In the quiet moments between rustling leaves,
They shared stories, where strength perceives.
The dragon's fire and the forest's gentle grace,
In the camping space, a connection to trace.

Trans Dragon tattoo

Through the embrace of starlight, where night descends,
They set up a fire, where stories blend.
Their dragon tattoos, reflections in the flames,
A testament to strength, where wilderness claims.
As the night wore on, and stars took flight,
They sat by the fire, spirits alight.
Wings stretched wide, scales so bright,
In the language of ink, a wilderness night.

Through the woods where moonlight gleamed,
They walked, their spirits forever esteemed.
Their dragon tattoos, in the moon's soft glow,
A symbol of strength, in the wilderness's flow.
Through the tapestry of strength and nature's design,
Two trans hearts found courage intertwined.
The dragon's wings and the forest's soft hum,
In the wilderness journey, where strength becomes one.

Trans Dragon tattoo

In the realm of self-discovery, a tale unfolds,
Of a soul transcending, a story yet untold.
In the heart's cauldron, where courage stirs,
A trans spirit awakens, where identity blurs.
Born from the fire of authenticity's breath,
A trans soul emerges, conquering death.
From shadows of doubt to a sunlit embrace,
A dragon tattoo adorns, a symbol of grace.

Trans Dragon tattoo

Wings of strength unfurl, scales shimmering bright,
A dragon's presence, a beacon in the night.
On the canvas of skin, an ancient tale is inked,
The dragon's embrace, where transformation's linked.
From the cocoon of fear to a skyward flight,
A trans soul soars, bathed in moonlight.
Each inked scale tells of battles within,
A testament to resilience, where life begins.

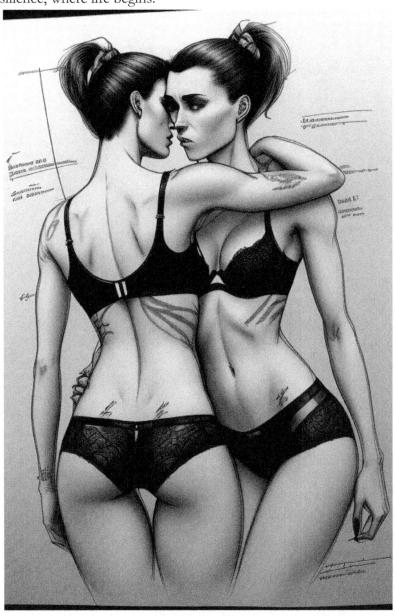

Trans Dragon tattoo

Eyes, deep as caverns, reflect starlit skies,
A gaze that pierces, where truth never lies.
In the dragon's tattoo, a narrative spun,
Of a trans journey, courageous and won.
Tail coiled around the past, scales reflecting pain,
A dragon's embrace, a shelter from disdain.
Horns, a crown of defiance, pierce the night,
A trans warrior's courage, an unyielding light.

Breath of flame, a symbol of power reclaimed,
A trans individual, strength unchained.
The dragon's tattoo, an emblem so grand,
A union of self, where destinies stand.
Through valleys of doubt, to mountainous peaks,
A dragon's tattoo, where vulnerability speaks.
In every swirl of ink, a chapter unfolds,
A saga of courage, where authenticity molds.

The dragon's wingspan, a shelter of might,
A trans heart beats, a rhythmic flight.
In the tapestry of ink, stories entwine,
A dragon's embrace, where spirits align.
So let the inked dragon, fierce and wise,
Guard the trans spirit, where strength lies.
A symbol of metamorphosis, fierce and free,
In the dragon's embrace, a trans symphony.

CHAPTER 10

A DRAGON'S ECHO

In the dragon's lair, where courage breeds,
A trans spirit dances, fulfilling its needs.
Scales shimmer with tales of battles won,
A dragon's tattoo, a radiant sun.
Through the valleys of prejudice, shadows of doubt,
A dragon's roar echoes, casting shadows out.
In the inked canvas, a metamorphosis unfolds,
A trans odyssey, where destiny molds.

Trans Dragon tattoo

The tail, a serpent winding through time,
A symbol of resilience, a journey to climb.
Coiling around scars, embracing each mark,
A dragon's embrace, where shadows embark.
Horns pierce the silence, a crown of defiance,
A trans heart beats, claiming self-reliance.
In the fire-breathing ink, a testament to might,
A dragon's tattoo, where dreams take flight.

Wings unfurl in the storm of societal scorn,
A trans soul rises, a new era is born.
The dragon's embrace, a sanctuary complete,
In the inked narrative, a heartbeat.
Eyes that gleam with the wisdom of stars,
A dragon's gaze transcends societal bars.
Through the mist of labels, the dragon soars,
A trans anthem, where acceptance restores.

Moonlit tales etched in the dragon's embrace,
A trans individual, finding their place.
In the dragon's roar, echoes of pride,
A symphony of authenticity, nowhere to hide.
Beneath the dragon's wings, a sanctuary found,
A trans spirit rising, breaking through the ground.
In the labyrinth of ink, a trans saga spun,
A dragon's tattoo, where identity is one.

Trans Dragon tattoo

Beneath the dragon's wings, a haven secure,
A trans heart beats, resilient and pure.
Scales tell stories, etched in vibrant hue,
A dragon's tattoo, a narrative so true.
Through valleys of judgment, the dragon soars,
A trans spirit rises, society ignores.
In the tapestry of ink, a saga weaves,
A dragon's embrace, where authenticity cleaves.

Trans Dragon tattoo

Tail wrapped around the echoes of the past,
A dragon's tattoo, a bold contrast.
Horns pierce through darkness, a beacon of light,
A trans anthem echoes, dispelling the night.
Eyes, a reflection of the dragon's might,
A trans gaze, piercing through the night.
In the fire-kissed ink, courage unfurls,
A dragon's embrace, where identity swirls.

Trans Dragon tattoo

Wings span wide, embracing the sky,
A trans journey, learning how to fly.
In the dragon's roar, echoes of strength,
A symphony of resilience, going to great lengths.
In the dance of scales, a symphony composed,
A trans spirit, no longer enclosed.
The dragon's tattoo, an armor adorned,
A declaration of self, no longer scorned.

Trans Dragon tattoo

Through the labyrinth of ink, a path well-defined,
A dragon's embrace, a spirit enshrined.
With every heartbeat, with every breath,
A trans individual, conquering life and death.
In the dragon's lair, where shadows part,
A trans spirit dances, a work of art.
Scales kissed by moonlight, tales of might,
A dragon's tattoo, a beacon in the night.
Through valleys of judgment, the dragon weaves,
A trans spirit rises, society deceives.
In the tapestry of ink, a tale is spun,
A dragon's embrace, where worship's begun.

Trans Dragon tattoo

Tail coils around the echoes of the past,
A dragon's tattoo, a symbol steadfast.
Horns pierce through darkness, a crown of pride,
A trans anthem echoes, nowhere to hide.
Eyes, reflecting the wisdom of stars,
A trans gaze, breaking societal bars.
In the fire-kissed ink, courage found,
A dragon's embrace, where worship's bound.

Trans Dragon tattoo

Wings span wide, embracing the sky,
A trans journey, learning how to fly.
In the dragon's roar, echoes of worship rise,
A symphony of bodies, a sacred guise.
In the dance of scales, a worship unfolds,
A trans spirit, a story retold.
The dragon's tattoo, an altar adorned,
A celebration of bodies, a love reborn.

Through the labyrinth of ink, a path divine,
A dragon's embrace, where bodies entwine.
With every heartbeat, with every breath,
A trans individual, embraced unto death.
Beneath the dragon's wings, where shadows flee,
A trans heart beats with a symphony.
Scales tell tales of bodies intertwined,
A dragon's tattoo, where ecstasy's defined.

Trans Dragon tattoo

Through valleys of judgment, the dragon soars,
A trans spirit rises, exploring new shores.
In the tapestry of ink, desire takes flight,
A dragon's embrace, where sexuality ignites.
Tail entwined with passion, a dance begun,
A dragon's tattoo, where sensuality's spun.
Horns pierce through shadows, a crown of grace,
A trans anthem echoes, in the sacred space.

Eyes, mirrors reflecting the allure,
A trans gaze, where beauty matures.
In the fire-kissed ink, passion's flame,
A dragon's embrace, where bodies proclaim.
Wings span wide, embracing the night,
A trans journey, where desire takes flight.
In the dragon's roar, echoes of beauty ring,
A symphony of bodies, a sacred spring.

Trans Dragon tattoo

In the dance of scales, a story unfolds,
A trans spirit, where desire molds.
The dragon's tattoo, an altar of pleasure,
A celebration of bodies, a love to treasure.
Through the labyrinth of ink, a path to bliss,
A dragon's embrace, where desires kiss.
With every heartbeat, with every breath,
A trans individual, an embodiment of depth.

Trans Dragon tattoo

In a world where stories unfold,
A trans soul, both brave and bold,
With inked scales, a tale is told,
No metaphor, just truths to hold.
Upon their skin, a dragon's trace,
A symbol of courage, in this space,
No hidden meanings to embrace,
Just a journey etched, face to face.

Trans Dragon tattoo

In every line, a history,
Of battles fought for liberty,
No veiled words, just honesty,
A body marked, a diary.
No metaphors to cloud the view,
Just raw emotions shining through,
In every shade of red and blue,
A story real, a life anew.

Trans Dragon tattoo

The dragon's eye, a fierce regard,
No hidden symbols, just regard,
Reflecting struggles, not discarded,
A mirror true, life's playing card.
Beneath the scales, a beating heart,
No need for metaphorical art,
Just a journey from the very start,
A testament to inner part.

Trans Dragon tattoo

Wings spread wide, a fearless flight,
No metaphoric veil in sight,
Just a will to live, to take the light,
Through the darkness of the night.
Oh, trans soul with dragon's ink,
No metaphors to make it sync,
Just a life story, link by link,
On your beautiful body's brink.

Let every curve, each subtle bend,
Speak of a journey, a soul on mend,
No need for metaphors to send,
The message clear, from end to end.
In a world where love is a sacred art,
Trans beauty is a masterpiece, a work of heart.
Their bodies, a temple, worshipped and divine,
Each curve and line, an invitation to intertwine.

In the quiet moments of intimacy's embrace,
Trans souls find solace, a sacred space.
Skin on skin, a communion profound,
A celebration of love, resounding sound.
To worship the trans form is to understand,
The strength it takes to make a stand.
In the face of judgment, they boldly rise,
Their bodies, a testament to love's reprise.

In the mirror, reflection of strength and grace,
Trans beauty shines in every embrace.
No need for judgment, just acceptance true,
Their bodies, a canvas of colors to view.
In the tenderness of shared breath and touch,
Trans intimacy becomes a sanctuary, a clutch.
No need for masks, no need to pretend,
In each other's arms, broken hearts mend.

Trans Dragon tattoo

So let us celebrate the trans soul,
Worship their beauty, make it whole.
In every gaze, in every caress,
Acknowledge the beauty, free from duress.
For in the worship of trans essence,
We find love's true omnipresence.
Their bodies, a shrine of courage and pride,
In the sacred space where love resides.

Trans Dragon tattoo

In a world where diversity takes its stand,
Trans beauty is woven, a tapestry grand.
Bodies unique, no two the same,
An equal part in life's vibrant game.
Intimacy found in shared connection,
A dance of hearts, a deep reflection.
In the silence of souls drawing near,
Trans beauty whispers, loud and clear.

Each form, a canvas of endless story,
A testimony to strength and glory.
No need for judgment, no need to weigh,
Let each individual path have its say.
In the quiet spaces of understanding,
Trans bodies speak, softly demanding
Recognition of their worth, untold,
In a world where acceptance can unfold.

Worship not mandated, but a choice,
To honor each person's unique voice.
In the realm of self-discovery,
Trans beauty thrives in autonomy.
 Beneath the crescent moon's soft glow,
Two souls collided, hearts aflow.
In a tapestry of ink and skin,
A dragon's fire, a butterfly's spin.

Trans Dragon tattoo

He bore a dragon fierce and grand,
In ancient ink, tales of a distant land.
Scales etched on skin, a fiery lore,
Yet in his eyes, a gentleness to adore.
She, adorned with a butterfly's grace,
In hues that painted an ethereal space.
Wings of freedom, delicate and bright,
A dance of colors in the quiet night.

In the coffee shop's dim-lit embrace,
Their eyes met, a serendipitous trace.
A connection sparked, unspoken and deep,
As if fate had secrets yet to keep.
The dragon whispered of strength untold,
Of fiery passions, of stories bold.
The butterfly fluttered, a dance so light,
In the language of ink, their worlds unite.

Together they walked through life's shifting scenes,
With dragon's courage and butterfly's dreams.
A fusion of tales on their intertwined skin,
A love story painted from within.
Through storms they weathered, hand in hand,
Their tattoos told a story so grand.
Of love's endurance, of whispers in the night,
In the canvas of life, they found their light.

In the dance of love, we find our way,
Trans bodies close, in the gentlest sway.
Kissing softly, a connection so sweet,
A love story unfolding, hearts in sync, complete.

Lustful whispers, desires take flight,
Sensual moments, in the soft moonlight.
Making love like a gentle stream,
Reaching peaks of pleasure, like a beautiful dream.

Our bodies entwined, a perfect rhyme,
Exploring each other, one heartbeat at a time.
Kissing like the breeze, so soft and light,
A symphony of pleasure, reaching new heights.

The passion unfolds, a story untold,
Love's tapestry woven, pure and bold.
In this dance of souls, an intimate treasure,
Our love story continues, an endless measure.

Under the stars, our bodies entwine,
Lost in the moment, everything aligns.
With every kiss, a promise we make,
A love so genuine, nothing's at stake.

Making love like whispers in the night,
In each tender touch, emotions take flight.
Reaching peaks of pleasure, together we soar,
A timeless dance, forever wanting more.

In the quiet aftermath, a tranquil glow,
Wrapped in love, we let the emotions flow.
This journey of passion, our hearts decree,
A love story written just for you and me.

Printed in Great Britain
by Amazon

40725422R00112